MW00962099

# The Fart That Saved the World

## The Deadly Field Trip

## by M.C. Gill

Copyright © 2017 by M.C. Gill

ISBN-13: **978-1547086344**

ISBN-10: **1547086343**

*For the two special people in my life, Nolan and Ashley. I couldn't have made this book without the humor and love from both of you.*

# BONUS – Free Audio Version of This Book

As a Thank You for checking out this farting adventure, we have included the audio book for FREE! If you want to listen to this funny adventure in audio form then just go to:

**www.FartingHero.com/FieldTrip**

(Only available for a limited time!)

## Other Books by M.C. Gill

The Fart That Saved the World (Book 1)

## Chapter 1
# My Butt Funk & My Best Friend

Hello there! My name is Lance and I have a problem with farting *lots* of farts, all the time. These aren't normal farts either. They are the most disgusting smelling anal screechers you could ever imagine. Close your eyes and think of the foulest odor in the entire universe (if you are having problems, my suggestion is the poop of an elephant that has eaten nothing but rotten eggs for an entire week, in the heat of summer). Can you imagine that gross a smell? Well, the stench given off by my butt rippers is 100 times stronger than any odor you could ever come up with.

And the problem with my butt blasters is not just the stench. My thunder from down under is so loud that it can be felt by those around me! When people hear it, they think that an airplane is flying above their head a little too close to the ground.

I have had these extreme anus issues for my entire life, and I'm quite embarrassed by them.

But things changed when I moved to my new school and met fellow sixth-grader, Aiden. He showed me that my farts were special and a thing to be proud of. We quickly became best friends and every day I marvel at how much of a genius he is and he marvels at my impressive butt bombs. We make a great team!

It was our teamwork that stopped the evil Dr. Deuce from unleashing a worldwide poo storm. No one else knows how close the doctor was to destroying the planet or that Aiden and I saved the world! And that's ok with us. Plus, without Dr. Deuce, I wouldn't have found the best dog in the world, my basset hound, Daisy.

But this story isn't about Dr. Deuce. That story has already been told. This story is about the second time that I had to use my backside rippers to stop evil from destroying this world. Lucky for me, Aiden was there by my side again to help me as good friends always are there when you need them.

This story is about how I used my farts to save the world!

## Chapter 2
## Show & Smell

I think that Daisy is the best dog in the whole world! While she isn't the brightest crayon in the box, or the sharpest tool in the shed, she brings me tons of joy. Before Daisy, I felt alone with my farting filibusters. But now she is by my side, breaking warm wind right along with me.

As soon as Daisy was mine, I wanted to show her off to everyone I knew! That is why I was excited to bring her into school when it was my turn for show and tell.

School has been pretty rough in the past few weeks, because I no longer had my Fart Blocker 1000 underwear. The FB1000 was an invention made by Aiden that helped block out some of the odors and sounds that came from my overly active anus. They helped me gain confidence in myself, since I was a little shy with my issue of farting grossly, loudly, and constantly. The problem is that the FB1000 was lost when Dr. Deuce kidnapped us. While I thought about asking Aiden to make me another pair, I didn't want to come across as greedy.

So, bringing Daisy into school was a bright spot for me during some tough times. Without the FB1000, I was always afraid of busting loose some skunk funk and causing the entire class to spew chunks all over each other (which has happened in the past). I was more anxious and shy than I had been since starting at this school at the beginning of the year.

"Hey, what's wrong?" asked Aiden on the morning of my big day of show and tell.

"I am just afraid that while I am standing up in front of everyone, I will let a fart loose," I confessed shyly.

"Just try to relax and not worry about the rest of the class. They are going to love Daisy because she is awesome!" Aiden reassured, trying to make me feel better. He was such a great BFF.

As class settled in, our teacher, Ms. Peach, calmed everyone down. I knew that show and tell was the first thing we did in the morning so I took a deep breath and tried to clench my sphincter from opening its mouth and talking during my presentation.

"Today, Lance has brought in his dog for show and tell," Ms. Peach announced to the class. "Lance, the floor is yours."

I nervously got up and walked to the front of the classroom. I could feel the farts gathering in the pit of my stomach with every step that I took.

Daisy was happy as ever to be walking up, knowing that she was about to be the center of attention.

"Hi everyone!" I announced nervously. "This is my dog, Daisy"

As I nodded toward the dog, everyone looked at her. Most of the kids seemed to smile at her and she looked like she was smiling back at them.

"She is a basset hound and has an incredible sense of smell!"

"Does she have an incredible sense of smelling *bad*?!" shouted a voice from the back of the room.

I cringed as I heard the voice, because I knew right away whom the voice belonged to. It was Todd, the class bully, who liked to pick on everyone, but especially me for my farting issues.

"Because the dog's owner, Flat-U-Lance, sure does stink!" Todd said, which made half of the class start laughing at me. The other half looked uncomfortable as they could sense that Todd's antics were embarrassing me.

Daisy walked over to Todd like she was going to address this situation herself. I was proud for a minute... until I saw that all Daisy was doing was lying down on Todd's shoes.

"Your dog likes me better than she likes you!" shouted Todd.

My belly started to rumble as my anxiety grew. Had Daisy really abandoned me for the class bully? This was unreal!

Daisy appeared to be sleeping at the feet of Todd, with her tail wagging fiercely. She seemed to be quite happy, which made me quite sad.

As I felt my tummy rumbling with the anxiety fart that was sure to be coming out at any moment due to my embarrassment and sadness, something unexpected happened.

While Todd sat there gloating and laughing at me, Daisy's tail managed to go under his pants leg, pulling it open wide. She then backed up to his leg, looked me in the eye, and farted the loudest dog fart ever heard in the history of mankind!

Todd's face turned from joy to confusion as he heard the sound and felt the heat of the butt buster that Daisy just laid on his ankle. Then, Daisy's big whiff of foul air traveled up Todd's jeans, through his shirt, and smacked Todd right in the face!

Todd screamed in disgust as he tasted the air that just came out of the dog. The class laughed at Todd as he tried hard not to get sick on himself.

Daisy stood up and strutted back to my side, so I could finish telling everyone about my awesome dog.

## Chapter 3
# PUFFERS

One day, Aiden asked me if I wanted to come over to his house after school. Of course, I said yes because he was my BFF, and hanging out with him was always a fun time. Plus, I was not nearly as nervous about my stink bombs when I was around him.

I knew something was different as soon as I got to Aiden's house that day because he had a wild grin on his face the minute he opened the door.

"What is going on?" I asked, smiling back at him. Smiles are infectious that way.

"I have been working really hard on a surprise for you and I finally finished it!" Aiden exclaimed with a light in his eyes.

"What is it?" I asked excitedly.

"I know you loved the Fart Blocker 1000 I designed for you," Aiden replied. "And I know how sad you were when that got lost at Dr. Deuce's fudge factory."

I thought fondly of the FB1000, which did give me more confidence back when I had it.

"Well, I have been working day and night to design and build a replacement pair. I now present the Fart Blocker *2000*!" Aiden exclaimed, handing me a box.

I was so excited! I quickly opened the box and pulled out the shiny pair of underwear. I don't think a kid has ever been *this* stoked about getting a pair of underwear in the history of the world.

"Now these are a bit different than the Fart Blocker 1000," Aiden said. "Actually, *more* better than different."

"How so?" I asked.

"Well, you know how the FB1000 only minimized the amazing powers of your farts?'

I nodded, wondering why he used the word "only". They didn't "only" do anything. They saved me from massive embarrassment from my massive explosions!

"Not only does the Fart Blocker 2000 prevent the smells and sounds from being as powerful, it doesn't let that power go to waste. It actually stores the fantastic powers of your flatulence inside this little canister!" Aiden said pointing to the small cylinder that was attached to the side of the shorts.

I was now a bit confused.

"Why does it do that?" I asked, trying to figure out this new contraption.

"Remember when Dr. Deuce was trying to use your fart power to destroy the world?"

"Of course." How could I forget?

"It made me think that *we* shouldn't be wasting your powers. You have an amazing ability, Lance. An ability that we don't quite understand, but we know it is more powerful than anything in this world."

I blushed at the thought of being some kind of superhero.

"Let's not waste it. Let's harness that power, in case Dr. Deuce comes back and we need to defend ourselves. Or in case we need to stop some other kind of evil force."

I didn't quite get what he was saying, but I liked the sound of it.

"That canister stores your powers and then you can use *this* to unleash them," he explained, presenting me with what looked like a pen.

"Am I supposed to write something down?" I asked, confused.

"No, this is the Phenomenal Unleashing Frequent Fart Evacuation Routing Shooter or PUFFERS for short. It may be small, but when connected to the FB2000 canister, it can shoot a bolt of concentrated fart power."

"How do I do that?"

"Just connect it, using this small cable, to the canister. Then point and click this button. It works just like a laser pointer but much more powerful."

"Wow!"

"The downside is that you only get one shot. One click takes all of the fart power stored up in the FB2000, and it will take another day or so for you to fart enough to recharge."

I took the PUFFERS in my hands and looked at it, mesmerized by what Aiden was saying.

Little did we know that within a few days, we would be saving the world again thanks to Aiden's new inventions!

## *Chapter 4*
## **The Farting Field Trip**

As our bus pulled up in front of the Great Lakes Botanical Gardens, my entire class was excited. Ever since this field trip was announced, we had been counting down to this day. I love the outdoors and nature, so the opportunity to go to a place with lots of plants was *extra* exciting to me.

Also, I had regained some of my confidence, since I was now wearing my new Fart Blocker 2000 underwear. Without the FB2000, I was sure that one belch from behind would kill many of the plants at the botanical gardens (I have a history of killing plants with my stink bombs).

Ms. Peach led us kids off the bus where we could take in the fresh air and enjoy being outside of the classroom for a day.

"I can't wait to see the butterfly exhibit!" said Aiden, as he was exiting the bus.

"I didn't know they had butterflies too! I only knew they have great plant exhibits," I said back.

"You two are a couple of nerds!" said Todd, pushing his way past Aiden and me. "This place is lame, but it sure beats being stuck in school all day. As long as I'm not supposed to learn things or write things, I'm happy to be here."

We followed Ms. Peach into an auditorium that was located near the entrance to the park.

After taking a seat, Ms. Peach stood in front of us, giving a hand motion to quiet us down. She was getting our attention so she could make an announcement.

"Children, before we go outside to see what Mother Nature has in store for us, the staff here at Great Lakes Botanical Gardens wants to show us a presentation."

"Lame!" sneered Todd, trying to be funny but coming across as more of an imbecile. Some of the kids snickered, but they all stopped as soon as Ms. Peach shot an annoyed glare in their direction.

The presentation was short and consisted of some intelligent looking people explaining details about plants, flowers, bees, butterflies and other things in nature that could be found in the botanical gardens.

While I was farting with excitement as I sat there, I almost forgot about my stomach issues, since the FB2000 was doing its job. The presentation explained that the scientists who study plants are called botanists, and one of the speakers, Dr. Green, was one of the top botanists in the world. Dr. Green seemed to know everything when it came to plants and it showed.

At the end of the presentation, Dr. Green said he had one more thing to say before we could continue with our day:

"In honor of the 100th anniversary of Great Lakes Botanical Gardens, we are hosting a special competition. I have been training three young botanists in the past few years and we have decided to give them a chance to show us their skills. Each of them has had the opportunity to grow special plants that they think will be a good addition to the gardens. Jan, Larry, and Patricia, come out here with your plants!"

Three younger looking people in lab coats came to the stage, each of them pushing a cart holding a planter with plants inside. I wasn't close enough to the stage to get a good look at the plants, which was frustrating because I really wanted to see them.

"The winner of this competition will get a cash prize of $5,000 AND their picture will be put on a large banner for everyone to see as they come into the gardens. This will make them famous!" Dr. Green shouted.

We all cheered in excitement.

"And the best part is that the winners are chosen by the visitors to the gardens. So, come up kids and take a closer look at the choices, so you can vote for your favorite plant."

Aiden and I jumped up immediately because we were super excited to be a part of picking the winner. We started picking up speed as we got closer to the stage.

"Boys, no running!" Ms. Peach shouted.

Just as we slowed down, a larger boy jumped in front of us.

"Yeah, no running," repeated Todd, in a voice that was mocking our teacher.

"Todd, get out of our way," said Aiden, as we tried to get past him.

"Yeah, we want to see the plants and place our vote," I said.

"I promise I will leave you both alone," Todd said, with an innocent smile, "...if you do what I say."

Aiden and I knew Todd was still mad about the incident where he tasted Daisy's backdoor breeze. We were happy he hadn't tried to do anything about it, but we quickly realized Todd was just waiting for the perfect time, which he apparently thought was *now*.

"What do you want?!" I asked, losing my patience, but also slightly afraid of what Todd wanted.

"Come over here and I'll tell you," Todd said, motioning us away from the crowd of the other kids. "It's an important secret and I don't want the teacher to know."

We looked at each another and knew that it was not a good idea to do what Todd wanted, but at this point, we just wanted it to be over with.

Reluctantly, we decided to follow him.

"Ok, we followed you over here. What do you want?" asked Aiden.

"I want you to pay for what you did to me!" grunted Todd, as he pushed us both hard in our chests, each one of his large hands powerful enough to knock us off balance. I fell backward fast and hard and I could tell that Aiden did the same. By the time we came to our senses, it was dark. I quickly realized that Todd had shoved us into what seemed to be a broom closet and closed the door.

As I jumped to my feet in an effort to escape the dark, stinky, tiny closet, I heard the click of the door being locked from the outside. Oh no!

## Chapter 5
# The Stench Wasn't Coming from Me (For Once)

"Oh no!" I yelped, panicked. "I think Todd just locked us in here!"

"Take a deep breath and try to relax," Aiden said, trying to calm us down. "We both know that if you get too anxious, then you will start farting up a storm. Even with the FB2000 on, the smell will start filling up this closet fast."

Aiden was right. I took some deep breaths, which is what I try to do anytime I am anxious or nervous. I say *try* because sometimes it's hard to remember that this basic technique will calm me down.

The breathing was working and I was thinking more clearly. And better than that, my stomach started to relax and I could feel that I wasn't going to blow up the closet with my fart power.

Now we needed to figure out what we were going to do to get out of the closet. Yelling wouldn't help because my excited class was loudly examining the plants on staget, trying to decide which one they were going to vote for. I was jealous that I wasn't out there doing the same.

"Maybe there is something that we can use to pry the door open," suggested Aiden.

"Good idea!" I said, while starting to feel around the closet. The darkness made it impossible to see anything.

"I think I found something!" gasped Aiden.

There was a loud clicking noise and the next thing I knew, the floor gave way underneath my feet. Aiden and I were suddenly tumbling down some sort of slide. I was very confused about what was happening and butt poppers started shooting out of me again.

After a few seconds, we both landed suddenly on a soft surface. The smell was overwhelming; I thought for a second that I had pooped my pants out of fear.

But I realized quickly that the stench wasn't coming from me. The strong odor was from the soft surface we were now lying on. It appeared to be some sort of mulch. I knew from helping my mom in the garden that mulch is a dirt-like substance that helps plants grow. I also knew that it was often made with the poop of cows or other animals, which is why we were now surrounded by a cloud of stench worse than even I was used to.

"Are you ok?" I asked Aiden as I stood up.

"Yeah, I am fine."

"Well, that smell is *not* me."

"I know. It appears that we landed in mulch." Aiden observed, smiling. I could see a bit clearer now, even though the room that we were in was not the brightest, but it was still better than that dark closet.

"What happened?" I asked Aiden.

"I must have activated some sort of secret switch which dropped us down here."

"Where do you think 'down here' is?"

"I'm not sure, but it seems like it is a secret place that we probably shouldn't be in," Aiden said, with a little bit of panic in his voice.

My relief from being out of the closet was quickly replaced with dread after hearing what Aiden had just said.

Our fears were confirmed when we heard the footsteps of someone approaching.

The face of a woman covered in dirt appeared in front of us.

"What are you doing down here?!" she screamed.

Before we could answer, we saw that she had a vial in her hand filled with a strange looking liquid.

"This is acid," she warned, looking at the vial. "Do what I say or I will throw it on you!"

## Chapter 6
# Dirty Doris Dankenstein

"Who are you and why won't you let us go?" I asked the woman who was holding us hostage.

After confronting us with acid, the dirty woman forced us into another room that looked like it was some sort of secret lab. Memories of being in Dr. Deuce's lab swirled in my head and made my stomach uneasy. My farts were out of control.

"My name is Doris Dankenstein, and I work here at the Great Lakes Botanical Gardens!" the woman announced. "And I'm not letting you go because I don't want you to ruin my special plan. You two have already seen too much!"

Doris pushed us to the corner of the laboratory toward two huge plants that were as tall as we were. The plants were as scary looking as they were tall, with what appeared to be large mouths that were constantly chomping away.

"W-W-What are those?" Aiden asked. We were both scared of whatever those giant plants were, especially since she seemed to be moving us toward them.

"Those are my creations. Aren't they lovely?" said Doris.

Whatever they were, they were definitely *not* lovely.

"I made those plants by crossing the species of different plants together. My goal was to take a Venus Fly Trap and make it larger. Wouldn't you say that I succeeded in my goal?" Doris snickered as she said this.

She grabbed ropes, made out of thick green vines, from the corner of her lab and used them to tie Aiden and me together, back-to-back.

"I also created these ropes by mixing together the strongest plants in the world. Trying to get loose from them would be a futile exercise."

"You seem very smart, ma'am," mumbled Aiden.

"Do not try to patronize me, boy! I *know* that I am smart! I am a botanist like this world has never seen!" shouted Doris.

"Sorry, I didn't mean anything by it," said Aiden looking down, afraid to meet her gaze.

"It's ok, boy. I'm sorry that I snapped at you," said Doris, her demeanor quickly switching from anger back to glee. "It's not your fault that I'm stuck down here in this pit. It's *their* fault!" Doris pointed up at the ceiling.

"Those people call themselves *botanists*! HUMPH! They don't know anything about plants! And they had the nerve to kick me out of the competition because they said my plants were evil!"

Doris appeared to be talking to herself as she said all of this, barely aware that Aiden and I were still in front of her.

"I am going to show them all by ruining their little competition! If they want to see the greatest plant in the world, then I am going to show it to them!"

Doris gestured to the planted pot sitting on a table in the lab. It didn't look like much, but Doris seemed to be quite pleased with it.

"This is the deadliest plant in the world! It might not look like much now, but as soon as I add my special fertilizer mixture, the plant will grow taller than the tallest building on the planet! It will grow and grow and grow, until it takes over this world and blocks out the sun!"

"Wouldn't that be bad for everyone?" I asked, my question snapping Doris back into realizing that we were still there in front of her.

"Of course! That's my plan, boy! I want everyone to pay for not recognizing that I am a genius! The entire planet will pay with their lives, leaving only me to live with my plant creations."

The thought of this turned my stomach. I had already been farting non-stop since we fell into this secret lab, but it stepped up to another level after hearing of Doris Dankenstein's plan of destroying the world as we know it.

I wish I wasn't wearing my FB2000, because I know the strong stench from my butt busters would have knocked Doris out cold. But even if that happened, Aiden and I would still be stuck here, tied together, guarded by the two large snapping plants next to us.

"You two stay put! If you try to make any sudden moves, then my giant snapping plants will eat you alive! Now is the time for me to unveil my deadly concoction and destroy the world! The world will never forget Dr. Doris Dankenstein; the greatest and last botanist to ever live!"

With that, Doris took her plant off the table and ran out of the lab.

Aiden and I were stuck, tied back-to-back, being guarded by two ferocious snapping plants, as Dr. Dankenstein was about to kill everyone we loved.

## Chapter 7
# Learning a New Skill

"If only I could reach the PUFFERS," I said, "Then we could kill at least one of those snapping things and get out of here."

Aiden didn't respond. This meant that his mind was already working hard on a solution to our problem.

"If only Daisy were here, then she would attack those evil plants and save us!" I proclaimed.

"That's it!" shouted Aiden.

This confused me because Daisy wasn't here, and we both knew that if she were here, she would probably be useless to help us. While she loves me, and is great, she is not much of an attack dog. Even though she would just be lying in the corner napping (and farting) if she were here, it would still have comforted me to see her one last time before the world was destroyed.

"Huh?" is the sound that came out of my mouth.

"Remember what Daisy did to Todd at school?" Aiden asked excitedly.

"Yeah, she ripped an unholy one right up Todd's pants leg; it was great!" I said, smiling at the memory. It was good to get my mind off the bad situation we were in even for one millisecond.

"Well, you can do the opposite of that. While your Fart Blocker 2000 does an excellent job of holding back and storing your farts, it is not airtight. If I made them airtight, they would explode and blow your butt off every time you ripped a big one," Aiden explained.

"OK," I said, trying to anticipate where he was going, while also getting more nervous hearing the plants around us snapping open and closed, like they were ready to eat us.

"I'm not 100% certain, but I *think*, if you are able to lift your leg high enough, you will break the seal on your FB2000."

The gears were turning in my head as his plan began to make sense.

"All you have to do is time a big juicy crunchy ripper to blast out the second you lift your leg and the fart should shoot right out of the bottom of your pants. If you can aim it at one of these snapping plant things, it should be enough to take it down. Do you think you could fart?"

We both already knew the answer to *that* question. I've been on the verge of crapping my pants since we got into this whole mess!

"Of course!" I shouted.

I started taking deep breaths in and out. We needed this fart to be a good one, not a tiny tooter, but more of a gigantic gasser. As I did my breathing, I could feel the air building in my anus; it took a lot of willpower to hold it all in until the right moment.

"Ok, I'm ready," I whispered, afraid that if I spoke too loud, I would accidently release the butt bubbles.

Aiden started counting, "1...2...3!"

As I heard the number three being said, I lifted my leg up as high as I could, aimed it the snapping plant and pushed out with all my might. I hoped that I didn't poop, but I had to do whatever it took to get the job done.

As soon as I pushed, I felt a wave of heat traveling down my leg and blow out the end of my pants. It sounded like a cannon had gone off as the stench bomb shot out. The force of the whoosh of toxic air pushing out of my pants leg knocked me back, pushing Aiden forward. Luckily, he was prepared for this and had his feet planted on the floor, so we didn't get pushed toward the second snapping plant.

After recovering from the blast, I looked over at my victim and saw that our plan had worked. The snapping plant was no longer standing straight. It had completely collapsed and looked much less green than it had seconds before.

"Yes! We did it!" I said to Aiden, who was unable to see since his back was still tied to mine. "Now let's get away from that other one."

I shuffled my feet toward the collapsed plant and away from the one that was still snapping in its planter.

"Let's go over there and see if we can sever these vines holding us together with the sharp edge of the table," Aiden suggested.

I looked over and saw the steel lab table in the middle of the room. We headed toward it and started rubbing the vine binding us together on the sharp corner of the table. It took some effort and a little time, but we were able to cut through one of the pieces of the vine, which unraveled the entire thing.

"Now we need to go warn the others about Dr. Dankenstein's evil plan to destroy the world!" I exclaimed, as soon as we were free.

## Chapter 8
# Banished to the Bus

With a little investigating, Aiden and I were able to find a ladder that took us out of the wretched lab of Doris Dankenstein. My guess is this is also how she escaped to execute her evil plan.

As soon as we exited the lab, we realized exactly where we were, which was right outside of the auditorium. We looked around, scouting for Doris, hoping we could stop her. We were also afraid, because we didn't know what she would do if she spotted us first.

Our goal was to find our teacher so we could explain to her the evil plot that we had learned about. People had to know, so they could stop Dr. Dankenstein from killing everything.

As we turned the corner around the building, we were both relieved to find Ms. Peach.

"Where have you boys been? We have been looking everywhere for you!" ranted Ms. Peach in a frenzy. She seemed really upset.

"She wants to destroy the world!" I yelped, gasping for air. I was out of breath from our quick escape.

"You know what? I don't care where you have been!" she said in a loud, demanding voice. "There is NO reason that you two should have left the rest of the group and you both know that!"

"But..." Aiden tried to say.

"There are no 'buts' Aiden! You boys are generally well behaved, so I have no idea what caused you to leave our group! We were in a panic looking for you! I almost had to call your parents!"

"Todd..." I was trying hard to explain everything, but my mind was racing with all the different things to say. It didn't matter, because Ms. Peach did not want to hear anything from either of us.

"Yes, Todd told me that he noticed you two sneaking away while the rest of the class was judging the plants." Ms. Peach said.

Aiden and I both gasped at hearing this. Todd had been the one who locked us in that closet and it's his fault that we were away from the group! The fact that he told this blatant lie to our teacher to get us in further trouble really steamed us.

"Your field trip is over! While the rest of the class continues learning about the wonderful things here at the botanical gardens, you two are going to be sitting on the bus." Ms. Peach said firmly, guiding us toward the bus.

"But, we must stop her!" I pleaded.

"Not one more word from either of you!" snapped Ms. Peach. "If I hear another peep out of you, then you are both going to be in even bigger trouble than you already are."

We didn't know what that meant, but we knew that there was no way of getting through to the teacher. She was very mad at us, and rightfully so. In her eyes, we had strayed away from the class and were missing for a while. I'm sure this scared her, and she felt she needed to teach us a lesson so we wouldn't do something like that again.

I understood all of this, but I didn't like any of it. It wasn't fair, because we *hadn't* done any of those things. We were the victims, both of Todd and Dr. Dankenstein. But none of that mattered now, because Ms. Peach needed to calm down before we could have any sort of conversation with her. And calming down was not something that was going to happen for quite a while.

Ms. Peach walked us to the bus, opened the doors, and motioned for us to get inside. We did as instructed.

"Do not even *think* about leaving this bus!" she ordered, before closing the doors.

We waited a few minutes after she left before talking to each other because we were afraid that if she heard us talking, then we might get into more trouble.

"What are we going to do now?" I asked Aiden.

"I don't know, but we better do it quick," he said.

We both stared out the window, trying to think of our next move.

Suddenly, we heard a loud noise followed by screaming.

I knew what that meant. It meant that the evil botanist had unleashed her evil plant and it was now growing large destroying everything. It meant that Dr. Doris Dankenstein was about to take over the world.

## *Chapter 9*
# We are Not Waiting Around for the World to End!

"**W**e must try to stop her!" I screamed aloud.

"We've got to get to that plant and stop it from growing and destroying the planet!" Aiden agreed.

I jolted as I remembered the PUFFERS that had been sitting in my pocket all day.

"Do you think this would work to kill the plant?" I asked Aiden, as I took the PUFFERS out of my pocket and held it up.

Aiden's eyes lit up, "I'm not sure, but assuming the canister is full from soaking in your ripe farts all day, it's our best hope at stopping that thing."

"Of *course* it's full! My butt has been going off like fireworks all day long!" I said smiling.

I attached the cable of the small PUFFERS to the canister and I felt optimistic; we *could* save the world (again).

"Now remember, you only have one shot with that, so be careful," Aiden warned me.

"I know. I'm going to make sure it counts," I said. "Let's go!"

We both headed toward the back of the bus and escaped through the emergency door located there. It's weird because I never thought I would be exiting a school bus this way. It's weirder that the two of us were rushing toward danger to try to save the world.

After getting off the bus, we ran in the direction of where all the chaos seemed to be happening, which was in the auditorium where we saw the presentation earlier. Entering the building felt like going into a burning house; part of me wanted to run away from danger, not toward it. But with great farting power comes great farting responsibility. My farts were the only weapon that could stop Dr. Dankenstein's evil plot.

As we got inside, we could see through all the chaos that Doris was on stage, laughing maniacally as her plant grew at a rapid pace. It had already overcome the entire stage with roots and vines, and was starting to overtake the people in the auditorium.

Dr. Green and the other three botanist contestants were tied up with the same vine rope hybrid that Dankenstein had tied us up with. She must have made a dramatic entrance that caused all the mayhem leading up to her fertilizing her plant and letting it take over the building.

"How close do I need to be for this thing to work?" I asked Aiden, holding the PUFFERS in my hand.

"Just to be safe, I would say that you should be pretty close," he responded.

That is not what I wanted to hear. I wanted to just shoot the thing from where we were in the back of the auditorium, but I also didn't want to miss my one shot.

"Then let's get up there and try to save the world!" I shouted over the noise in the room.

I was confident that we could do this quickly. We started running toward the stage, trying to avoid the large vines growing around us. The vines were starting to overtake some people and pin them down; we didn't want to be one of its victims.

"How did you two get in here?!" shrieked an evil voice from the stage.

She spotted us! My confidence sank into my belly and came out of my bottom in a fury of flying farts.

Doris Dankenstein put on a gas mask and headed toward us in a hurry. I don't know why she had a gas mask, but it felt like she was prepared for us. Did she know about my farting abilities? It didn't make sense.

As she approached us, she noticed the PUFFERS in my hand. I hoped she would think it was just a pen, since that is what it looked like.

I didn't want to waste the blast on her because I needed it to stop her growing plant. Also, I didn't want to hurt her too badly. She is a person, even though a quite evil one, and I wouldn't want to kill her with the power of my pooper gas.

"Do you think you are going to stop me with a pen?" I heard her mumble through her gas mask. Then it sounded like she was doing that evil laugh thing again.

Before I could respond, she smacked the PUFFERS out my hand, and knocked me to the ground.

Aiden's reaction to this was to run away from both of us. I guess he was just too scared and I didn't blame him, but I thought he had more courage than to just abandon me.

I had no idea what to do. I couldn't try the fart-kick again because it would be useless with her wearing a gas mask. I felt useless myself.

As people around me screamed while being taken over by this plant, which was becoming as large as the room, it seemed like the world was about to end.

## *Chapter 10*
## **The Fart That Saved the World (again)**

Lying on the ground, I turned my head looking for something, *anything*, I could use to try to take down Dr. Dankenstein. She was way bigger than me, but I figured that I must try to do something. If I didn't, then her evil plant was going to take over everything.

As my eyes darted around the room, looking for something to help, and hoping that Doris did not hit me again, I saw him. He was running around the outer walls on the other side of the room, trying not to be overtaken by the growing plant. Aiden!

I knew what he was doing. He didn't run away out of fear. He ran away to get out of sight of Dr. Dankenstein, because he knew that tactic was our best shot at stopping her. And now he was about to execute his plan as he continued scurrying around the border of the room, closer and closer to getting behind Doris.

I knew that I must engage her so she wouldn't notice the sneak attack that Aiden was about to execute. I looked her directly in the eyes.

"This plan will never work because you aren't a good enough botanist. Dr. Green is *so* much better than you could ever become!" I said with fury. I knew that she would have to defend herself, even to me. She couldn't stop herself.

Her eyes widened in anger. "How dare you?!" she screamed through her gas mask. "You don't know anything about AHHH!"

Aiden had made his move and had jumped on her back as fast as he could. She was shocked by what was happening and started swatting at him. Lucky for him, she couldn't quite reach his smaller body as it hung from her back with his arms wrapped around her shoulders.

"Lance, get ready!" he shouted at me.

I saw his hand reach toward her gas mask and I knew what that meant.

I jumped up from the ground and bent backward.

"Now!" exclaimed Aiden.

I breathed in a big inhale as I shot my leg in the air trying my hardest to aim at the face of Dr. Dankenstein.

"In with the good, out with the bad," I calmly intoned to myself.

As I exhaled the air from my lungs, my butthole shot out a stinky current of air that could only be described as a fart dart. The heat that I felt told me that it was a truly stinky butt buster that would do the damage that I wanted. In fact, for a minute I thought that I hot fudge caked my pants, but that was a risk that was needed for this particular moment.

Aiden pulled the gas mask off her face just as he heard the loud noise erupt from my pants; it sounded like a broken trumpet being played at full volume.

Dr. Dankenstein's eyes rolled in the back of her head and I knew my fart had met the mark of her nostrils. She instantly passed out and fell down. Lying on top of her was my BFF, Aiden, who had saved me.

"Aiden, come on. We need to kill this plant!" I said nudging him.

As I rolled him over, my worst fears were realized. My stink bomb had hit him in the face too. Just like Dr. Dankenstein, I knew that he would be fine in a few hours once he woke up from getting hit by my funky crack whistle.

"Sorry," I said to Aiden, even though he couldn't hear me at that moment.

I searched around looking for the PUFFERS because I still had a job to do. I found it on the floor and attached it to my shorts again. I took another deep breath trying to relax myself. I knew that I still needed to get close to the plant to kill it.

As I got closer and closer to the plant, I had to dodge the vines and limbs that were constantly moving toward me. It was like the plant knew where to find its victims and was trying to take the life of everything around it. I hoped that Ms. Peach, Dr. Green, and everyone else were still alive and doing ok under the weight of the now ginormous plant.

I only got knocked down once as I headed toward the plant, but it wasn't enough to hurt me or pin me down.

Finally, I was as close to the main part of the plant that I could get. I looked at the PUFFERS in my hand and prayed that it would work.

I pointed it at the plant and clicked the button.

I knew that I hit my mark as I saw the giant plant and all its vines instantly turn to dust.

And that is how I USED MY FARTS TO SAVE THE WORLD!

# *Epilogue*

A few days after the field trip, we returned to the Great Lakes Botanical Gardens to help clean up the mess left by Dr. Doris Dankenstein and her evil plant.

Doris was arrested after the incident and we hear she is doing better after going to therapy in prison.

Aiden and everyone else involved were ok, which was lucky. The police say that the plant was on the verge of knocking down the entire auditorium building before it died, which probably would have killed everyone inside. The police don't know what killed the plant because there were no witnesses. I don't plan on telling them anytime soon either, because I'm not interested in the kind of attention that would bring. Plus, how do I explain that my farts saved the world?

So, we all came back to clean the place up, but this time I was able to bring Daisy since it wasn't an official school event. That dog loves being outside and she loves hanging out with Aiden and me.

As we picked up dead pieces of plant and dirt and helped put the place back together, Daisy's nose led her away from us.

"Daisy, where are you going?" I asked her as she moved farther and farther away from where we were.

We ran to catch up to her, but when we got close I could tell that there was no stopping her. She was on the scent trail of something and she wasn't going to stop until she found what her nose was looking for.

We followed Daisy as she led us up to the stage where the evil plant had been. She stopped as her nose touched a large bag. Apparently, the bag is where the trail ended. She sat, looked at the bag, and started growling and barking at it.

"Calm down girl," I said soothing her, leaning down to look at the bag.

The bag looked plain on the outside, but as I turned it around, I noticed a note attached to the back.

My eyes widened with disbelief as I read -

**HERE IS THE SPECIAL FERTILIZER I MADE FOR YOU TO EXECUTE YOUR PLAN. GOOD LUCK – DR. DEUCE**

# About the Author

M.C. Gill loves two things: comedy and his son Nolan (not in that order). That's why he decided to write books about a boy like Nolan who saves the world with his farting powers.

M.C. and Nolan live in Dayton, Ohio where they enjoy spending time telling jokes and playing board games together.

91154522R00039

Made in the USA
Columbia, SC
13 March 2018